# The Musical Life
# of
# Gustav Mole

Illustrated by Kathryn Meyrick

This edition published exclusively for
Discovery Toys, Inc.
by Child's Play (International) Ltd.

**Lucky the mole born into a musical family!**

Rock-a-bye, Gustav, don't you cry.
Mother will sing you a lullaby.
Father will play the violin.
Sleep, baby Gustav, breathe out and breathe in.

**A musical home is never dull!**

Three happy animals, one, two, three!
Playing a trio – Do you see?
Someone is clapping.  Yes, it's me!

Father plays the violin,
Mother plays the oboe.
Frog plays the cello.
He's a very fine fellow.

## Musical moles learn fast!

Four happy animals
Play a string quartet.
I conduct them with my rattle,
But they aren't at all upset!

Father and Hedgehog on the violin.
Mouse with a viola under her chin.
Frog is on the cello.
He's a very fine fellow.

## The more the merrier!

The more we are together,
The merrier we get!
Five happy animals
Playing a quintet.

Father and Mother on the violin.
Hedgehog at the piano.
Badger plays the double bass.
Frog is on the cello.
There is no doubt, he's a very fine fellow.

**Music is made to make friends!**

All the animals have brought their musical toys
to Play School. We sing, dance and have fun.

Spike and I play drums! My cousin plays castanets and
trumpet! It is deafening! Really good music!

Mother shows us how to make our own instruments.
She says it will help us to understand music better.
Froggie shakes beans-in-a-jar.  Spike blows the bottle flute.
Little Badger plays the pan-and-spoon.  I play the bottle-phone.

At school, we learn to play real instruments.

This is Badger
on the triangle.

This is me
on the recorder.

This is Hedgehog
on the xylophone.

This is Mouse
on the drum.

This is Frog
on the tambourine.

**Music is for singing!**

We learn to sing together in the choir.
We sing all our favorite nursery rhymes,
like *Pop goes the Weasel, Old Macdonald,
There was an old Lady, This old Man* and
*There were ten in the Bed.*

**Music is for everyone!**

Once a year, all the animals get together for the Village Music Festival. Some play and some listen.

Frog and Hedgehog rehearsed for weeks!

The highlight is the Flute and Harp Concerto,
played by Frog's cousin from the Frogharmonic Orchestra
and the famous flautist, James Badger.

**Music is for dancing!**

On my birthday, my parents take me to the Barn Dance.
My paws are carried along by the catchy rhythm
of Big Badger's piano accordion.  We dance until we ache!

Then we listen to Fox playing the guitar and singing
sad folk songs. My eyes fill with tears.

"Father and Mother," I sob, "I want to be a *real* musician!"

Father gives me
my first lessons
on the violin.

"You will
have to practice
every day!" he says.

"In music,
there isn't
any other way!"

"Now, do like I do!"

So, I practice hard.

I do like he does.

Why is he making
that face?

"You are practicing TOO hard!" my friends shout
above the noise.

But I take no notice, and in the end
I win a scholarship to the Music Academy.

I want to learn all about the orchestra,
so I go to a concert performed
by the Famous Frogharmonic.

I will never be able
to play like them, I think.

Not in the percussion.

Not in the wind section.

Those Frogs have a special gift
the rest of us can only dream about.

Not in the brass.

Not in the strings.

I don't stay sad for long.
I go to hear the Birds and Reptiles Jazz Band.
Parrot plays the trombone, Satchmo Snake the trumpet
and Tree Frog the drums. Cockatoo is on the keyboard.
Alligator is on the double bass. Toucan plays the banjo.

Tickle those ivories, Cockatoo! Dig that crazy Toucan!
Twist and shout, Snake! See you later, Alligator!

The very next day, we form our own jazz band!

Put your hands together, please, for Badger
on the tenor saxophone!  For Fox on the double bass!
For Hedgehog on the drums!

And last but not least, for the leader of the band,
the great jazz violinist, Gustav!

I return to my studies.

I am still determined
to be a virtuoso.

I give my first recital.
I feel wonderful.
But something is still
missing from my playing.

My tutor says,

"You were good, Gustav,
very good, but —
I'm sorry —
you will never be a Frog!"

One day, a poster appears on the Academy notice board.
The Great Maria Frog is coming to sing Carmen
at the opera house! Her picture makes me weak at the knees!
I must have tickets. So must the others.

We are all madly in love.

The passionate music
flows over us.

Carmen is,
well,
overpowering. . .

But
in the chorus
stands
the cutest
little Mole.

My heart and my head are filled with music.
In my room, I begin to write.  I have found my musical self.

I am going to be a composer.

Beneath the balcony of her room, I serenade her
with my *Lover's Lament!* I know she is there.
I heard her giggle! What bliss!

Suddenly, my happiness, my head and my violin are drenched
with cold water.
She does not love me! I flee in despair!

My life is over. I hurry to the music shop to sell my violin.
But my friends won't let me.

"Don't do it, Gustav! You need your music more than ever, now,"
they plead.

They are right.  My violin is all I have left.
My broken heart will never mend!

One day, I am sitting sadly in the snow,
playing my *Lover's Lament.*

Suddenly, she is there!
She has heard the tune.

"Gustav, you short-sighted silly!
Maria was jealous!
*She* threw the water!"

"Marry me!" I cry.

"I will! I will!
Of course I will, silly!"

Music has brought us together again.

A few weeks later.

I wish you could have been here, at our musical wedding!

My musical life has been very happy.
I have enjoyed every sort of music, listening and playing,
dancing and singing. Now I am a successful composer.

And we are very happy! All seven of us!

**Lucky the mole born into a musical family!**